60072697

DI761272

CITY CENTRE CAMPUS
SUCCESS CENTRE

You can renew your books by
Phone: 02920 406545
Email: successcentre@cavc.ac.uk
Text: LZN to 07537 402400 with your ID

CARDIFF AND VALE COLLEGE

I Gwyddno,
Seiriol
ac Einion

First edition: December 1988
Second edition: August 1993
© Y Lolfa Cyf., 1988

Illustrations by Helen Holmes

ISBN: 0 86243 125 5

Printed and published in Wales
by Y Lolfa Cyf., Talybont, Ceredigion SY24 5HE;
phone (0970) 832 304, *fax* 832 782.

PREFACE

'Y Mabinogion' is the term given to a collection of eleven folk tales written in Mediaeval Welsh which have come down to us in two early manuscripts, the White Book of Rhydderch and the Red Book of Hergest. I offer part of each tale as a foretaste for children of what they may read in their entirety some day.

This adaptation into English is based on my volume Mabinogi'r Plant, published in 1986 by Y Lolfa. I am grateful to Helen Holmes for preparing the illustrations, and to Elan Closs Stephens for editing the English text.

RHIANNON IFANS

CONTENTS

RHIANNON AND THE MAGIC STALLION

Pwyll, Prince of Dyfed, had a very comfortable court at Arberth. While there one lovely June, a splendid feast was prepared for him and his men. They all ate far too much and eventually went out for a walk in the fresh air.

Behind the court stood Arberth Hill, and they decided to climb to its summit. By the time they arrived there, they were all out of breath. When they had rested awhile, one of the men said, "Lord Pwyll, did you know that this hill is a very special hill?"

"O yes," said Pwyll, "it's very pleasant here, and the scenery is marvellous."

"No, no, I meant special in a magic way."

"O? How is that?" asked Pwyll.

"If a prince sits on the summit, it will be impossible for him to leave without one of two things happening to him. He will either be injured, or he will see a great wonder."

"It's impossible for me to be injured when I have my men around me," said Pwyll, "but I wouldn't mind seeing something wonderful. I'll stay to see what happens."

As they were talking a woman passed by, riding a white stallion. She wore a beautiful dress of gold brocaded silk. "I wonder who she is," Pwyll mused. He questioned his men but no-one had any idea who she could be. "Someone had better meet her," Pwyll said, "to solve the mystery."

One of his men got up but by the time he had reached the road, she had passed by. The man followed her but since he was on foot it was impossible to catch up with her. The more he hurried the further away the woman rode. "It's useless for anyone to follow her on foot," he said to himself, and so he returned to Pwyll with his story.

"Fetch a steed from the court—the fastest one there, and then you'll be able to catch up with her easily. Hurry!"

He ran to the court as fast as his legs would carry him. He quickly chose the fastest steed in the stable and galloped after the woman. On reaching the plain, he dug his spurs deep into the horse's side. The more he spurred his steed, however, the further away the woman rode. Before long the poor horse was almost on its knees, its back running with sweat and drivel dripping from its nostrils. When the rider realised that the horse was tiring, he slackened his pace and returned to Pwyll and his friends who awaited his news.

"Lord Pwyll, it's pointless for anyone to follow that woman. There isn't a faster steed than this one in all the land, but it didn't get near her stallion. It's impossible to catch her."

"There must be a magic meaning to this," said Pwyll. "This must be the

wonder that I was supposed to see. Let's return to court and decide how to solve this mystery."

They spent the day thinking about the strange woman on the white stallion and teasing one another about her. The next day they were still talking about her and eagerly wanted to know whom she could be. After eating, Pwyll called the same group of men and asked them

to return with him to the summit of Arberth Hill. They were delighted. "Bring with you the fastest stallion in the kingdom," said Pwyll to one of his young servants.

When they reached the top of the hill they were very excited. What if the woman didn't come? But as they were talking about her, the woman appeared riding the same stallion, wearing the same dress, and travelling along the same road as on the previous day. "Here she is! The one we saw yesterday! Hurry, servant, we want to know who she is!"

But before the servant could sit in his saddle the woman had passed. The servant followed her thinking that he would overtake her quite easily. But, no! He struck his steed and it galloped like the wind. To no avail. She moved further away from him by the minute, although she didn't appear to be moving at all quickly. What a wonder the whole thing was.

When he returned to Pwyll, his master had a word of comfort for him.

"You tried your best, but I could see that there was no use you following her.

I'm sure she's on some errand, but she's too obstinate to tell us about it."

Having returned to his court that evening, Pwyll decided that he would unravel the mystery, come what may. He, personally, would follow the woman as soon as she appeared again.

The next day he took the same group to the summit again. He had with him his own steed and his spurs and he was all set for a race. Soon after reaching the summit of Arberth Hill the woman appeared in the distance, wearing the same dress, and riding the same stallion.

"Bring me my horse at once," he called to his servant. "I'm going to follow her." He jumped onto his steed. He galloped after her—galloped and galloped and galloped. But in vain. It was impossible to catch up with her.

"Lady!" Pwyll called out at last. "Wait for me! For heaven's sake, wait!"

"Of course I'll wait for you," she called out happily, "and it would have been far better for your horse had you asked me to wait a good while since."

She started chatting easily with him. "It was you I came to see Pwyll. My name is Rhiannon, daughter of Hefëydd the Old. My father is forcing me to marry someone I don't like. I wondered whether you'd marry me instead?"

"Well, upon my word!" said Pwyll, his head spinning. "Rhiannon," he said, "here's my answer. If I had my pick of all the women in the world, I would choose you."

And that is how Rhiannon chose her husband.

BRANWEN IN IRELAND

Matholwch, king of Ireland, married Branwen, princess of the Island of the Mighty, at Aberffraw. They went to live in Ireland and Branwen became a favourite amongst all the courtiers. Within the year a son was born to her and she named him Gwern son of Matholwch.

But soon after this time, her subjects heard of the insult which Matholwch had suffered in the Island of the Mighty at the time of his wedding. Efnisien, Branwen's step-brother, had maimed Matholwch's horses by cutting off their lips, their ears and tails. Although Matholwch had been given a strong horse instead of each injured steed, and much gold in addition, Matholwch's men forced him to seek revenge.

He decided to send Branwen to the kitchens to cook for the court members and told the butcher to box her ears each day after he had finished hacking the meat. This continued for three years. In order to prevent Bendigeidfran her brother from hearing of this indignity, all ships were banned from leaving Ireland for the Island of the Mighty.

Branwen had one friend and one only, a starling. It stood at her side while she baked bread, and Branwen taught the bird Welsh, telling it about her brother. One day, Branwen wrote a letter to Bendigeidfran complaining about her punishment. She tied it to the bird's wing and sent it to the Island of the Mighty.

The bird searched for Bendigeidfran and found him at a conference in Caernarfon. The bird ruffled its feathers and showed Bendigeidfran the letter. Bendigeidfran was very sad on reading it, and set sail at once for Ireland.

Of course Matholwch knew nothing of this visit. One morning, Matholwch's swineherds had the shock of their lives as they tended to the pigs on the seashore. They saw a forest in the sea and a mountain next to it with a lake on either side of the mountain; all these were moving quickly towards Ireland. The swineherds ran to Matholwch as

fast as their feet would carry them but he found their story quite incomprehensible. He sent for Branwen in case she could understand them.

Branwen understood perfectly. "It's Bendigeidfran. He's coming to avenge this insult," she said. "The trees that you see are ships, and the mountain is my brother. He's a giant. The high ridge is his nose, and the two lakes on either side of the ridge are his eyes He must be very angry."

Matholwch took fright and decided that the only possible course of action was to escape over Shannon and destroy the bridge to prevent anyone from following him. And so he did. When Bendigeidfran reached Shannon's banks there was no bridge. "No matter, I'll act as a bridge," he said. Since he was a

giant he was able to lie across the river; his forces walked across him to the safety of the other side.

Immediately, Matholwch's men raced to Bendigeidfran seeking peace. They gave their word that the kingship should be given to Gwern, Branwen's son. But that wasn't enough for Bendigeidfran, and it was decided that he, Bendigeidfran should be crowned King of Ireland, and that an enormous house be built for him, one so big that he could enter through its door. He had never before lived in a house because they were all too small for him.

Bendigeidfran was greatly pleased and a feast was prepared for all the soldiers. But the Irish had a plan. They wanted to kill the army of the Island of the Mighty. They nailed a sack to each

pillar in the house and hid an armed soldier in each one.

When Efnisien entered the house and saw the sacks of hide he was very suspicious of them.

"What's in this sack?" he asked one of the Irish.

"Flour," he said.

Efnisien trussed the sack and realised that there was a man inside it. He squeezed the man's head so hard that Efnisien's fingers met through the man's skull in his brains. He did the same thing to each sack.

When the guests arrived at the banquet, Efnisien created greater chaos by taking Gwern's feet and throwing the boy headlong into the flames. Branwen tried to save him by leaping into the fire

but Bendigeidfran grasped her firmly, for fear that she too would burn. Then everyone in the house began to fight like lions.

The Irish had a cauldron, the Cauldron of Rebirth. When one of them was killed he was put into the Cauldron and by the next morning he would be alive again, although he would not be able to speak. The warriors of the Island of the Mighty had no such cauldron and were therefore losing the battle.

When Efnisien realised what was happening, he squeezed amongst the dead bodies of the Irish in order to be thrown into the Cauldron with them. Once in the Cauldron, he stretched his body until the Cauldron split four ways and was totally worthless. Efnisien was killed instantly. Bendigeidfran was badly injured by a poisonous spear, and only seven men from the Island of the Mighty survived the fighting.

Bendigeidfran commanded his men to cut off his head and carry it to London to be buried. The seven men, Bendigeidfran's head, and Branwen sailed back to the Island of the Mighty and came to harbour at Aber Alaw in Talebolion. They rested there awhile. Branwen looked back towards Ireland with great sadness and then at her own country. "Son of God," she said, "woe is me my birth. Two good countries have been ruined because of me." At

that, she sighed wearily, and her heart broke because of her great sorrow. She was buried there, on the banks of the river Alaw, in Anglesey.

MICE! MICE!

Manawydan and his wife Rhiannon, and Pryderi and his wife Cigfa, had settled in Dyfed. The four were the best of friends. One morning Pryderi and Manawydan decided to hunt, so off they went. When their hounds reached a certain copse, they bristled with fear and ran back to their masters. "I wonder what's in that copse to frighten these dogs so," wondered Pryderi, and he and Manawydan went to see.

Like lightening, a white wild boar rushed out of the copse and the dogs attacked him. Pryderi and Manawydan

followed the hunt until they came to a big castle; the boar disappeared into it, quickly followed by the hounds.

The two men had an uneasy feeling about the castle. No buildings had ever been seen there before and now this splendid castle had appeared from nowhere. They watched the castle from a hilltop and listened for some sight or sound of the dogs. Nothing was seen or heard of them, not even the tip of their tails. At last, in the peace of the evening, Pryderi said to Manawydan, "I'm going to the castle to search for the hounds."

"That's not a very wise thing to do," said Manawydan. "I'm sure it's a trick."

But Pryderi went just the same, and Manawydan returned home.

As the day drew to a close without sign of Pryderi returning to court, Rhiannon insisted upon going to the castle in search of him. The castle gates were open and she hurried inside.

When she saw Pryderi she was horrified. He stood very still on a slab of marble, his hands glued fast to a beautiful vase. Moreover, he could not speak. She ran to help him and immediately the same thing happened to her. The two

remained there until nightfall, when a dense mist fell over everything. At that, they heard a peal of thunder, and suddenly, the castle disappeared, taking Pryderi and Rhiannon with it.

When Cigfa learned of these happenings, she cried bitterly, but Manawydan comforted her and promised to take care of her. But without hounds, they could not hunt for food so they had to leave for England to earn a living and to make enough money to buy a load of wheat to bring back with them to Dyfed.

Once home, Manawydan tilled the ground and sowed wheat in three fields, and that was the best wheat that anyone ever grew. When harvest-time came the corn was ripe and golden, and Manawydan said, "Tomorrow, I will harvest this field." That evening he returned to Cigfa a very contented man. He slept peacefully and dreamt of a full rickyard.

The next day he walked out jauntily, with every intention of reaping the first cornfield. But when he came to the field, a bitter disappointment awaited him. The corn stalks had been stripped bare. There was not one ear of corn left on any of them. What a dreadful mystery. He hurried to the second field to see how it had fared and was greatly cheered to find the cornfield a rich, golden growth.

"Thank goodness for that," said Manawydan relieved. "I'll harvest this field tomorrow morning, first thing."

Since there was nothing more he could do that day, he went home from the fields to Cigfa, a less contented man than he had been the previous evening, and his sleep was less peaceful.

Early next morning he hurried to the second cornfield intending to reap the corn, but another disappointment awaited him. Exactly the same thing had happened to his second field. Not one ear of corn remained on the stalks. He hurried to the third field. The corn there stood strong and ripe. "I must keep watch tonight to discover who is stealing my corn," said Manawydan to Cigfa when he returned to court. "The thieves are sure to return again tonight."

That night he hid behind the hedge to keep watch on the field. At midnight a mighty noise boomed over the land and a plague of mice, so many that no man could count them, rushed into the field, each one stealing an ear of corn before escaping. Manawydan was furious. He tried to kill them, but couldn't. He managed to catch one pregnant mouse, tied it in his glove, and took it home intending to kill it in the morning.

The next day he took the mouse to the top of Arberth Hill but when he was ready to hang it, a poor clergyman came to him offering him a pound for letting it go. "No, I'm going to hang it," said Manawydan and the clergyman went away.

As he was securing the crossbeam, a priest on horseback came up to him offering him three pounds for freeing the mouse. He refused once more. The priest went away and Manawydan made a noose around the mouse's neck. Everything was ready.

As Manawydan drew up the mouse to be hung, a bishop with his retinue came to him offering him seven pounds for releasing the mouse. When Manawydan refused he was offered twenty four pounds. A fortune! But no, he would not release the mouse.

"What will you accept instead of it?" the bishop asked.

"Before I release this mouse I must have Pryderi and Rhiannon back. I'm sure it was you who tricked us."

Immediately, Rhiannon and Pryderi appeared and the man, Llwyd son of Cilcoed, promised that he would not cast his magic spell over Dyfed ever again. The mouse was released and Llwyd touched it with his wand. It turned into a beautiful woman. Who was she? She was his wife.

LLEW LLAW GYFFES'S SECRET

Arianrhod had two sons, a fair-haired boy called Dylan, and a newborn baby. When the time came for Arianrhod to hold office at court, she gave her children to others to bring up and the little baby, Llew Llaw Gyffes, became great friends with Gwydion.

Gwydion was a very special person.

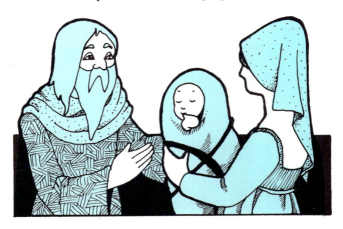

He could enchant, and cast spells. Llew Llaw Gyffes's mother hated Llew. She had vowed that Llew would never take up arms or have a name, but Gwydion managed to secure both in spite of her. Arianrhod was so angry and hated Llew so, she pledged an oath that no woman on earth would ever marry Llew. Poor soul. He was the most handsome youth in the world and he yearned for a wife.

Gwydion and Llew went to see Math son of Mathonwy, prince of Gwynedd, to complain about Arianrhod and to ask his help. How could Llew win a wife when no-one on earth was willing to marry him? They considered this problem for a long while, and at last decided on a plan of action. Gwydion and Math gathered oak blossoms, broom flowers and meadowsweet, and conjured into being a beautiful maiden, a woman of magic. She was the most

beautiful woman that mankind had ever seen. She was named Blodeuwedd and very soon she and Llew were courting. They married and went to live at Mur Castell in the uplands of Ardudwy.

One day, Llew went for a walk as far as Caer Dathl to visit Math. While Llew was away Blodeuwedd heard the sound of a horn outside the court and saw a tired stag going past, hounded by dogs and huntsmen. When she sent a servant to ask who they all were, the reply was, "Gronw Pebr, Prince of Penllyn, and his men." The company hunted, killed the stag and fed the hounds until night closed in. Blodeuwedd felt obliged to invite the company to

spend the night at court.

They accepted and were heartily welcomed. Gronw took off his armour and when Blodeuwedd and Gronw looked at each other they could not hide the fact that they were in love. They stayed together for three nights, plotting the death of Llew Llaw Gyffes on his return.

Blodeuwedd knew that it would be difficult to kill her husband; there was some mystery concerning the way that he would die. She and Gronw decided that the best way to discover the secret would be for her to pretend that she was anxious for Llew's safety, and that she

wished to know his secret in order to safeguard him against any possible danger.

"Don't worry," said Llew. "There's only one way of killing me. The killer must fashion a spear during Mass on Sundays and spend a year doing so. Then, I must wash on a river bank in a bath with a roof to it. If anyone strikes me with the spear while I have one foot on the bath and the other on a goat, I will die."

Blodeuwedd passed on the message to Gronw Pebr and immediately he began to prepare a spear. A year to the day, it was ready. Blodeuwedd persuaded her husband to show her how he would stand on the day when he would be killed, and he did so. Gronw Pebr was hiding on Bryn Cyfergyr nearby. He arose from his hiding-place and took careful aim. He hurled the poisonous spear with all his might and struck Llew in his side. His scream was terrifying.

Llew was transformed into an eagle and flew away.

Gronw and Blodeuwedd were delighted and in no time at all they were married. But Math and Gwydion mourned for Llew, and Gwydion set off in search of him. He journeyed through Gwynedd, and Powys far and wide, until one night he took lodging at the house of a serf in Maenor Bennardd in Arfon.

When the swineherd returned home,

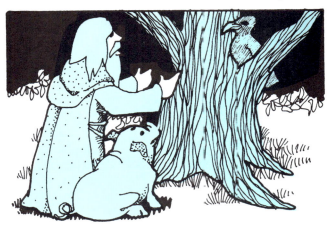

Gwydion heard from him that every day one sow escaped from the sty. Gwydion decided to follow it on the very next day. He followed it upstream to the Nantlle Valley where the sow stopped to graze rotten meat, and maggots. There was an eagle on the treetop above her, and Gwydion sang *englynion* to entice it down. Could it be Llew? At last it flew down on Gwydion's lap and Gwydion touched it with his wand. Indeed, it was Llew. But he was a pitiful sight. He was nothing but skin and bones. Gwydion took him to Caer Dathl to be healed.

In a year's time he was completely fit and well, and the time had come to punish Gronw and Blodeuwedd. When Blodeuwedd heard of this, she escaped to the mountains with her maidservants. They were in such fear of Gwydion that they walked quickly on—looking backwards instead of looking where they were going. No-one saw the great lake which was before them and all except

Blodeuwedd fell into it and drowned.

Now she was at the mercy of Gwydion. "I'm going to turn you into an owl," said Gwydion, "and you will not dare show your face again during daylight hours. The other birds will hate you and beat you at any chance. That will be your punishment." And so, Blodeuwedd was transformed into an owl, and disappeared into the twilight, screeching madly.

By now, Gronw Pebr was so afraid, he offered Llew much gold, silver and lands for his forgiveness and pardon.

But Llew would not listen. "You must stand in the same spot as I stood when I was struck by the spear, and I will stand on Bryn Cyfergyr. Then you must allow me to hurl a poisonous spear at you as you did to me."

Gronw had no choice but to agree. But he was allowed one concession. He was allowed to place a smooth stone from the river bank between himself and Llew. Llew aimed his spear carefully. He hurled it with such force, it went through the stone and through Gronw's backbone. It killed Gronw instantly.

LLUDD AND LLEFELYS

every May Eve. It was such a dreadful

scream it sent an eerie terror through every heart; men turned pale and felt faint; women miscarried; children lost their senses; the animals, the land and the rivers dried up completely.

The third plague was famine in the king's courts. The cook prepared splendid feasts which filled every storehouse, but they could only keep as much as they ate on the first day. No-one could understand this at all.

King Lludd anguished over the three plagues until at last he convened the noblemen of his kingdom to unravel the mystery. They suggested going to France to Llefelys in case he could solve their problems. So they prepared a fleet and off they went.

Llefelys sailed out to sea to welcome Lludd; they embraced each other but couldn't chat openly in case the Coraniaid overheard them. Llefelys fashioned a long horn of bronze, and they spoke through that. But the demon of the horn created trouble between the two brothers. However, after washing the horn with wine, they could speak unhindered.

Llefelys was indeed able to solve each problem. He had certain insects that he would give Lludd and if he retained some to breed and pulped the rest in

water, he could rid himself of the Coraniaid for ever. He was to fake a truce between his nation and the Coraniaid. When all had assembled in one building he was to spray the magic water over all, regardless; the Coraniaid would be

poisoned but his own subjects would remain unharmed.

"As for the scream," he said, "it's the dragon from your kingdom fighting a foreign dragon, and screaming a direful scream. Look for the island's centre spot and dig a pit there." Lludd looked at Llefelys with respect and listened intently. "Then place a cask of the best available mead in the pit and spread a silk cloth over it. Keep watch and when you see the dragons begin to fight, be very careful. They'll rise up in the air, fighting in the form of dragons, but when they tire of fighting they'll change

themselves into piglets and rush towards the cloth. That won't hold their weight of course and they'll fall into the cask and drink it dry. When you hear them grunt in their sleep, wrap them in the cloth, put them in a stone coffer and bury the coffer securely in the earth. While buried so, they'll never again plague the Island of Britain."

Lludd listened agog to his younger brother, while he went ahead to explain the cause of the third plague.

"A magician is stealing your food and drink by casting a spell over everyone and sending them to sleep. You, and no-one but you, must keep watch over your feasts, and in case he should succeed in lulling you also to sleep, make sure that you have a bathful of cold water nearby; you can jump into it when you feel sleepy."

Lludd was overjoyed. His problems were solved and he set sail for Caer Ludd in good heart. He mashed the insects in water and the Coraniaid were killed without more ado, every last one of them, and without injuring a single Briton.

Lludd carried on successfully. Having buried a cask of mead at the centre point of the island, he caught the two dragons and buried them in the most secure stronghold in all Eryri, Dinas Emrys.

His next task was to keep watch over

his feasts, but at about the third watch of the night he heard pleasant music and singing and he was almost lulled to sleep. Were it not for the bath of water, he would have slept soundly. He saw an armed man carrying a hamper come in to steal the food. Lludd was furious and the two fought until their swords

sparked fire. Lludd was the victor and from that moment onwards he ruled over the Island of Britain in peace.

MACSEN'S DREAM

Macsen Wledig, Emperor of Rome, was a wise and handsome man, highly esteemed by all. One day he held an assembly of kings, and he and thirty two other kings decided to hunt in a valley near Rome.

Macsen hunted in the valley until

midday. The sun shone high in the heavens and as the day wore on he became very sleepy. Soon, he decided to rest. His servants formed about him a wall of shields set on spear shafts to ward off the sun, and placed a shield burnished with gold as a pillow under his head. In no time at all, Macsen was fast asleep. Then he began to dream a very strange dream.

He dreamt that he was travelling

through a valley and following the river up to its source. Eventually he reached the highest mountain in the world. When he had crossed it, he journeyed through the most fertile regions that man had ever seen. As he approached the sea, he came to the mouth of a wide river. There he saw a large city and at its centre was a castle with towers of various colours.

He noticed a fleet in the river's mouth, the largest anyone had ever seen. In the middle of the fleet there was one special ship which was much more majestic than all the others. He saw himself walking its decks, the ship setting sail, and he sailing away! He sailed far across the seas and soon came in sight of the most beautiful island in the whole world.

Having journeyed across the island to its furthest reaches, he saw a great castle. It had a splendid hall. The roof

and doors of this hall were of pure gold, and its walls of brilliant gems.

Beside one of its pillars he saw a man who's hair was turning grey. The man sat on a throne, and before him on a golden-red throne sat a young woman. Such a beautiful woman! No-one had ever before seen a more beautiful woman than she. She arose from her throne and came towards him. He embraced her, and as their cheeks touched, the barking of his dogs awoke Macsen from his dream. Life was so uninteresting when he was awake. He had fallen in love with the beautiful woman in his dream. But who was she?

The Emperor was sad for a whole week. He had no desire to drink wine or to drink mead, nor had he the least wish to listen to songs or to listen to any other entertainment of any kind whatsoever. He only wished to sleep, because each time he slept he saw the young

woman of his dream, and when he was awake there was nothing on his mind except wondering where her home could be.

One day, on the advice of his servants, he assembled the wise men of Rome to tell them why he was so sad. Macsen told them of his dream and shared his grief with them.

Their counsel was that he should send messengers to all parts of the world to search for the woman he had seen in his dream. And so he did. But in a year's time they returned to Macsen having discovered nothing of the woman's whereabouts. The Emperor was very sad and was afraid that he would never hear of her again. His servants told him he should walk once again along the way that he had dreamed of.

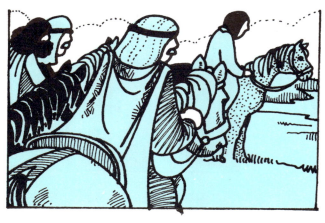

Instead of going himself, Macsen sent thirteen men along the river bank and across the mountain to the city by the river's mouth. There, they saw the wonderful ship amongst the world's largest fleet. They sailed on it to the

Island of Britain and crossed the island to Eryri. They could see Môn opposite them, Aber Saint, and the castle by the river's mouth.

On entering the castle and seeing the hall and the grey-haired gentleman, they saw the young woman. They approached her, bowed before her and greeted her as 'Empress of Rome'. She supposed that they were mocking her but when they explained the story of the dream, she said, "If the Emperor loves me so much, tell him to come here to look for me himself."

The messengers returned to Rome, travelling night and day, buying new horses when their horses failed. How thrilled Macsen was on their return! He rewarded the messengers, and they immediately agreed to lead the Emperor to the woman he had seen in his dream.

They came to the Island of Britain and there in the castle of Aber Saint, he saw the woman. He greeted her and embraced her, and she agreed to marry him. Her name was Elen.

Elen asked the Emperor to build three large castles for her. The most important was to be in Arfon, and the other two in Caerllion and Caerfyrddin. Elen then demanded wide roads to link her castles.

While Macsen was in Wales, a new Emperor was crowned in Rome. He sent Macsen a message threatening to kill him if ever he returned to Rome.

Macsen did return, however, conquering France on the way, and laid siege to the city of Rome. He remained there for a year until Elen's brothers came to his assistance with an army from Wales. Could they conquer Rome?

The height of the ramparts of Rome were measured during the night and carpenters built ladders to climb over them. Before long Rome was conquered and the new Emperor killed. Macsen and Elen claimed victory over the city and were grateful to the warriors of Wales for their assistance in battle. What better than a feast to celebrate?

RHONABWY'S
DREAM

Rhonabwy was on one of his campaigns with his friends. Ond evening, he went to seek lodgings at the house of Heilyn Goch, but on arrival he saw that it was a dirty old place. There were

holes in the floor and holly stumps everywhere. Even worse, when Rhonabwy stepped inside the house he was up to his ankles in cow-dung. When he entered the main hall he could see dusty, bare dais boards, and an old hag keeping watch over the fire. When she felt cold she threw a lapful of husks on the fire until the smoke and dust overcame them all. When they tried to chat to her, she answered them drily and rudely. Then, the owners of the house returned and they were no better.

After a supper of barley-bread, cheese and milk, a fearful storm blew up forcing Rhonabwy and his friends to stay the night. There was nothing for them to lie on but a bed of dusty, flea-ridden straw-ends and they had a greyish-red coarse blanket, full of holes, to throw over it. Over that blanket was laid a ragged coverlet, and at the top of the bed a half empty pillow covered with a filthy pillowcase. His friends were so tired they slept there and then in the midst of the fleas and every discomfort. But Rhonabwy couldn't sleep.

Eventually he slept on another dais, on a yellow ox skin, and dreamed a

dream. He saw a fair-haired youth on a yellow horse riding towards him. What

a sight! The horse's legs were green!
The rider wore a tunic of yellow silk and

carried a sword with a golden hilt to it.
He wore a mantle as yellow as the
flowers of the broom with fringes as
green as the leaves of the fir trees. The
rider looked awesome; Rhonabwy and
his friends were so frightened of him
that they fled. The rider pursued them,
and when his horse breathed out it blew
the men away from him, and when it
breathed in, it pulled them to his chest.
It was impossible for them to escape so
they begged the rider for mercy. "Of
course," he said, and they became
great friends.

The rider was called Iddawg the

Embroiler of Britain. As they travelled
together, Iddawg explained who each
knight was as they passed by, and who
was at the head of each army. Soon,
they happened to see Arthur and
Owain; they were playing chess on a
silver board with gold pieces on it.
While they were playing a young squire
came out of a white tent with a red top
to it. On the tent was the image of a
black, black serpent with red, venomous
eyes in its head, and a flame-red tongue.

"Arthur's soldiers and squires are
quarrelling amongst themselves and
fighting. Their commotion is upsetting
your ravens," said the squire. Owain
asked Arthur to prevent them, but he
refused.

In a while another youth came to warn Owain about the ravens but Arthur took no notice of him. They finished their game and began another one. As they played, another squire came up to them looking very angry. "Do you know that the most notable ravens have been slain and that those still alive have been badly wounded? Not one of them can lift its wings six feet from the ground."

But Arthur ignored him and said nothing to his men.

So Owain asked the squire to raise a standard at the spot where the battle raged at its worst, and so he did. Then a terrible thing happened; nothing of its kind had ever been seen before.

As the standard was raised the ravens

rose viciously into the sky. They drew on their strength and swooped down in one flock upon the men who had been ravaging them. They carried away the heads of some, others' eyes, others' ears,

the arms of others, and took them up into the air. There was a great commotion. The ravens were beating their wings and cawing frenziedly, and the men were screaming aloud as they were maimed and killed. Arthur appealed to Owain to prevent the ravens from killing his men. He would not, but went on with his game of chess. The ravens continued to maul the soldiers, dropping them to the floor in pieces. The noise of the cawing and crying was terrible.

Suddenly a rider wearing a helm of

gold with sapphire stones in it came towards them. On top of his helm was the image of a lion with its fiery red

tongue stretched a foot out of its head and its eyes red and venomous. The rider had a message for Arthur; his squires and soldiers had all been killed by the ravens. Owain seemed as if he hadn't heard a word that had been said.

In a while another rider brought the same message but no deliverance came although Arthur appealed to Owain to control his ravens. Arthur was furious. He grabbed the chess pieces and crushed them to dust. At last, Owain commanded that the standard be lowered. There was peace throughout the land immediately.

When Iddawg had explained to Rhonabwy who all the riders were, bards came to sing to Arthur and they were very melodious songs. No-one could understand their meaning except for Cadriaith, but they all knew that they were meant in praise of Arthur.

Then, twenty four asses arrived, carrying gifts for Arthur all the way from

the Greek Isles. The commotion they created was so great that Rhonabwy awoke from his dream. He was still lying on the yellow ox skin and had slept for three days and three nights. To be honest, he was glad to be back with the living, what with the ravens and fleas and all!

THE OLDEST
ANIMALS IN THE
WORLD

The giant Ysbaddaden Chief Giant had a beautiful daughter whose name was Olwen. Culhwch wanted to marry her. That was no great surprise. Many others had cherished the same thought before him, but Ysbaddaden was such a fierce giant, he had killed every man who had come to see her. One poor lady had lost twenty three sons, all for the love of Olwen.

Olwen wore a mantle of flame-red silk, rubies and costly pearls about her neck. Whoever saw her was sure to fall in love with her. Wherever she walked, four white trefoils grew in her footstep. That is why she was called Olwen, which means White Track.

One day, Culhwch walked into

Ysbaddaden's fort. He had had to kill nine gatemen and nine frenzied mastiffs before gaining entrance. Very soon he realised why the giant was against Olwen marrying anyone. The reason was that the minute she acquired a husband, the giant would die. Obviously Ysbaddaden wanted Culhwch dead but although he hurled a venomous stone-spear at him three times on three different days, he failed to kill him.

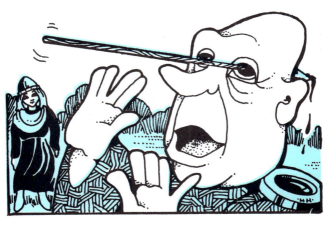

Culhwch and his companions caught the spears and hurled them back. They pierced Ysbaddaden with the first spear through the ball of his knee, with the second through his breast, and with the third through the ball of his eye so that it came out through the nape of

Ysbaddaden's neck.

The giant had to think of another way to prevent them from getting married. He set Culhwch a host of very difficult tasks and told him that he could marry Olwen after completing them.

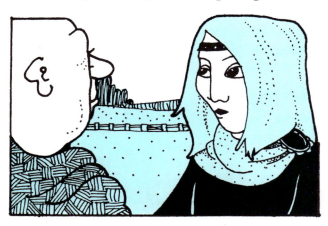

The tasks he set were so difficult, he was sure Culhwch would fail. One of these was to take the blood of the Black Witch, still warm, and take it to Ysbaddaden. Another was to find Mabon son of Modron. Modron was a man who had been taken from his mother's side when he was only three nights old. No-one knew where he was, nor even whether he was still alive. Culhwch accepted every challenge, saying: "You think these tasks are difficult.

I think they are easy."

Culhwch went away to begin his tasks. He decided that, first of all, he would search for Mabon son of Modron. He took Gwrhyr Interpreter of Tongues with him since he could speak every language. He could even speak to some animals and birds.

First, they asked the Blackbird of Cilgwri whether it knew anything of Mabon's whereabouts. The Blackbird said, "When I came here as a young bird, every evening I used to pick at a

smith's anvil. By now it has worn away. In all that time, I have heard nothing of this man. I wonder whether the Stag of Rhedynfre knows anything about him?"

He guided them to the Stag of

Rhedynfre and asked him whether he knew anything of Mabon son of Modron. "I have been here for many years,"

the Stag said. "When I first came here, there was only one tree growing here— a young oak sapling. That grew into an oak with a hundred branches to it. After that it fell, and today there is left only a red stump. So you can see how long I have been here. But in all that time, I have not heard a single word of Mabon. But the Owl of Cwm Cawlwyd is older than I. Perhaps it would know something. Come with me."

On they went until they came to the home of the Owl of Cwm Cawlwyd. "If I knew the least thing about him I would tell you," said the Owl. "When I

came here first this was a wooded valley
but settlers came here and cut down the
trees. A second forest grew. This is the
third and you know how slow trees are
to grow. Much, much time has passed.
My wings are mere stumps, but no, I
know nothing of Mabon son of
Modron. During all this time I have
heard nothing of him. But I do know
the oldest animal in the world, and the
one who has travelled furthest, the

Eagle of Gwernabwy. He ought to
have seen or heard something of him on
his travels. Come with me." They
followed the old Owl. Their hearts beat
aloud with excitement.

"When first I came here," said the
Eagle, "this stone was so high, I could

peck at the stars when I stood on it. By now, I've stood so much on it, it's worn down to the breadth of a man's fist. That's a long, long while but I have heard nothing of Mabon in all that time. However, I have a suggestion. I tried, once, to catch the Salmon of Llyn Llyw for my lunch, but it fought back so fiercely that I only just managed to escape. We have made our peace since then. If he knows nothing of Mabon, then no-one on earth knows anything. The Salmon of Llyn Llyw is your only hope.

And indeed, the Salmon knew exactly where Mabon was being held captive. It was in Caer Loyw. The Salmon had heard Mabon wailing and groaning behind the prison walls.

A large army was gathered to save Mabon. Whilst they were fighting, Mabon escaped on Cai's back. He was in too much pain to move an inch of his own accord. Culhwch rejoiced that he was able to return home, and to bring Mabon with him, a free man.

His success encouraged him to accomplish his other tasks and, yes, he succeeded in solving them all. Ysbaddaden's head was cut off and set on a bailey-stake. Culhwch and Olwen were at last free to marry.

THE MAGIC WELL

When Arthur was at home in Caerllion on Usk he was as happy as any king. On a day of leisure, when the knights were at their ease and the handmaidens sewing near the window, Owain suggested that Cynon should amuse them with a tale, a tale of the most wondrous thing he knew.

And so, Cynon began to tell them about his travels in the furthermost reaches of the world. He described how he came to a very beautiful valley at the end of the world. There was a large castle in the valley. Cynon boasted that when he reached the castle, two dozen of the prettiest maidens he had ever seen had come to serve him and to see to his horse and armour. Nevertheless he had

decided to move on.

At daybreak the following day Cynon set off on his travels and eventually came to a clearing in the wood. What a wonder! The clearing was full of wild animals and in their midst was a huge black man sitting on a mound and holding an iron rod in his hand. He held sway over every hair on every animal's back.

This man directed Cynon to a very peculiar well. Next to it was a marble slab and the man told Cynon to throw a pitcher of water over the slab. He would then hear a great noise and a cruelly cold shower of hailstones would fall on him. Then the sun would shine and the birds start singing. That was strange enough. Stranger still, a knight in black

would fight him.

Cynon was not afraid of anything dead or alive, so on he went to the fountain and threw a pitcher of water over it, without hesitation. Everything happened as he had expected: the noise and hailstones, the sunshine and birds. And, yes, the black knight appeared. He attacked Cynon and threw him off his horse. Cynon was very lucky to escape alive.

"That's the strangest tale I know," said Cynon to the company, "and I'm pretty sure that no-one was such a failure as I was when I fought the black knight."

"I'd like to see the fountain you speak of," said Owain, "so that I too can have this strange experience."

The following morning Owain rode away in search of the fountain. He travelled far and wide over desolate mountains to the furthermost reaches of the world until, at last, he came to the fountain in the valley of wonders. When the birds had sung, a knight appeared and they fought viciously. Owain struck the knight boldly, split the man's helm and mail-cap, and broke his skull.

The black knight fled. Owain was after him in a trice. He pursued him until they came to a large, shining castle. The black knight disappeared into the castle but the large wooden portcullis was let down as Owain followed him in so that Owain's horse was cut in two halves. Owain couldn't move. He would surely be caught.

He was in a real predicament until a young maiden whose name was Luned passed by. Luckily for Owain she agreed to help him escape from the guards. She possessed a stone which would make Owain invisible and in no time at all they were safe in a large, pleasant loft which was beautifully appointed.

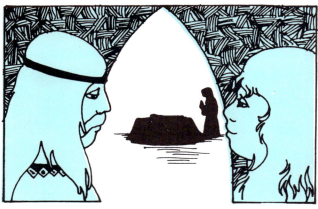

Owain bathed at leisure and rested, but on awakening he could hear the cries of lamentation of a funeral procession passing by. The black knight, the nobleman who owned the castle, was dead. As he watched the funeral, Owain noticed a very beautiful woman among the mourners, and fell in love with her at first sight. Luned warned him that she was the Lady of the Fountain, the black knight's widow. "She won't want you of all people, that's certain."

Despite this, Luned offered to woo the Lady of the Fountain on Owain's behalf. When Luned came to her the Countess was angry with Luned for not coming sooner to sympathise with her in her grief. They quarrelled and did not speak to each other for a while.

Luned was a very clever woman. When, at last, she was reconciled to the Countess, Luned suggested that the Countess should look for another husband to assist her in defending the fountain. She insisted that he should be one of Arthur's knights. She offered to go herself to Arthur's court to seek a husband for the Countess, and was given permission to do so. Luned hid in

the loft, of course, with Owain until enough time had passed for her to have come back from Arthur's court.

In a while Luned brought Owain before the Countess. Unfortunately the Countess soon saw through the plot, since neither looked like travellers. She guessed that this was the man who had killed her husband. Despite that, she decided to marry Owain for the sake of her kingdom.

Meanwhile, Arthur's courtiers were sad. Not one of them had seen Owain for three years. They decided to follow him along that same wondrous way. Cai asked to be the one who would joust with the black knight, and so it was agreed. By then, of course, Owain was the Knight of the Fountain, and in

ignorance, he threw Cai, his friend, off his horse with the butt of his lance.

Gwalchmai was next in combat, and they fought fiercely until Gwalchmai's helmet turned off his face and Owain realised that he was fighting his fellow knights. Fortunately, they had understood who was who before things had gone too far. Arthur and his knights were persuaded to ride with Owain to the Castle of the Lady of the Fountain.

Owain knew that Arthur would come in search of him one day and had prepared a feast for him in readiness. It had taken three years to prepare the feast and they all enjoyed the food and drink of that banquet for three whole months. Then Arthur returned to his court and Owain accompanied him.

Owain was to pay dearly for neglecting Luned and the Lady of the Fountain, but that is another story.

PEREDUR BECOMES A KNIGHT

A long time ago Earl Efrog held an earldom in Northern England, and he had seven strong, healthy sons. Although his subjects gave the Earl many precious gifts and much money, he earned more wealth than that at jousting tournaments, and in battle against his enemies. Each time he won a jousting match, he won a small fortune, and he regularly stole kingly treasures from his enemies.

But as so often happens to those who constantly go into battle, he was killed, he and six of his sons. This was a very sad time for his wife, and she mourned in deep anguish for her husband and children.

But she had a seventh son, a boy

named Peredur, the youngest of the family. Peredur was too young to understand even the basic principles of warfare, otherwise, quite possibly, he would have been killed like his father and brothers.

Peredur's mother was a wise woman. After much deliberation she decided that the best course of action for the sake of her son and kingdom, would be to flee with Peredur to a wilderness, a desolate, uninhabited place where she could bring up her son in peace. There she could prevent him from concerning himself with warfare. Above all else, she wished to prevent him from becoming a knight.

She took only quiet, contented people with her for company, people incapable of combat or war. She hoped that Peredur would never hear of horses or arms in case he set his heart on such

things. She was desperate not to lose her one, remaining son.

Peredur played every day on his own in the forest, throwing holly darts. One day, when he was in the forest, he noticed that two of his mother's goats had drawn near to two hinds, animals that he had never seen before.

The boy marvelled that they had no horns since each goat had horns. He thought that they must be wild goats; perhaps they were two of his mother's goats that had been lost for a long time and had therefore lost their horns. He

ran after them and was strong enough
and agile enough to drive the goats and
hinds into the goat-pen at the far end of

the forest.

He returned home exhausted and
complained to his mother of the trouble
he had had in driving the goats home
that evening. When his mother saw the
hinds, she was full of secret wonder that
Peredur was strong and agile enough to
pen them. He had the makings of a great
knight, and his mother's heart ached at
the thought.

In a few days, Peredur and the Countess saw three knights on horse-back
riding along the bridle-path on the
fringe of the forest. They were Gwalchmai
son of Gwyar, Gweir son of Gwestl

and Owain son of Urien.

"Mother," said Peredur, "who are they?"

"Angels," she said.

"I'd like to be an angel," said Peredur. He went towards the bridle-path to welcome the knights and to speak to them. He was as happy as a sandboy in their company.

"Peredur, did you see a knight pass this way today, or possibly yesterday?" Owain asked him.

"I don't know what a knight is," replied Peredur.

"We are knights," Owain said.

"I'll tell you if you answer my questions," said Peredur.

"Of course," said Owain.

"What's this?" asked Peredur, pointing to the saddle.

"A saddle," Owain said.

Peredur asked about everything, he was so keen to see their tackle, their garments, their arms and horses. He asked the name of each piece, how it all worked, how to use every part. Owain answered him in detail and explained carefully to him all that he wanted to know.

"Thank you," said Owain. "Yes, I saw a knight pass by and I too intend to be a knight from this minute. I will follow you to the ends of the earth."

Peredur returned to his mother and told her of his intention. Poor woman! She fell to the floor in a dead faint.

But Peredur was determined to become a knight, come what may. He

chose a horse for himself, a bony, piebald nag they used for carrying firewood and food to their home in the wilderness. Peredur placed a basket on it for a saddle and worked a harness of withes for it.

When he returned to his mother, the Countess was just coming out of her faint. She accepted that she had no choice but to let Peredur have his own way and to become a knight. She gave him good advice and away Peredur went on many exciting exploits, and brought honour and renown on his name until the end of his days.

GERAINT SON OF ERBIN AT A TOURNAMENT

One morning, Gwenhwyfar, Arthur's wife, slept and slept. When she awoke Arthur and his knights had gone hunting, and there was nothing to be done but follow their tracks and try to catch up with them.

She took her handmaiden with her. As the two women travelled, they saw a young and noble knight riding in the same direction. He was Geraint, one of Arthur's knights; Geraint also had slept until late and was searching for his lord.

As the three travelled onwards they saw a dwarf riding on a sturdy horse, another man riding a charger and a woman in a robe of gold silk travelling together. Gwenhwyfar was greatly excited and wanted to know who they were.

She sent her handmaiden to question them. When the dwarf saw her draw near he waited for her but when he had heard her question he refused to tell the maid who his fellow-travellers were. "Since you are so rude I'll ask the knight myself," said the maid and she turned her horse's head, fully intent on approach-

ing the lord and lady to question them.

Before she could move from the spot the dwarf struck her across her face with his whip. Blood streamed from the wound and the maid fled to Gwenhwyfar, crying in pain. Geraint was angry with the dwarf and challenged him.

Exactly the same thing happened to

him. He was struck so hard that the blood stained his mantle red. He set his hand on the hilt of his sword intending to kill the dwarf but there was no point. Geraint's weapons were poor ones and the knight on the charger would avenge his dwarf's death immediately. Geraint returned to Gwenhwyfar.

The three travelled on to the next town and found lodgings with an old man and his wife. The old couple had a beautiful maid who was very graceful although she wore a tattered gown and a worn, threadbare mantle. The maid waited on them and they ate their fill of good food and drink.

The dwarf and his companions were also staying in the same town. Geraint learned that the knight on the charger

was called the Knight of the Sparrowhawk, and that a tournament was being
held the following morning. A large
crowd was expected and it was thought
that a considerable number of knights

would joust for the prize.

Each knight brought with him the
lady he loved best in the whole world,
and the Knight of the Sparrowhawk
came with his lady-love. He had already
won the sparrowhawk for two suc-
cessive years and should he win it for the
third time, the title and honour was his
for ever.

Geraint was unhappy at this state of
affairs and talked about it all with the
old man.

"If you are ready to joust for your

love you may borrow my armour and my best horse. Who is the lady you love most in the world?"

Geraint had no young lady but he

thought quickly:

"I'll take your maid as my lady if I win this contest. Thank you for offering me your armour. I'll accept them gladly, but not your horse, thank you. I'm more used to my own horse."

The next day, before dawn, all four were up and about and by daybreak they were standing in their places on the meadow bank. The contest was about to begin.

They heard the Knight of the Sparrowhawk calling for silence, and claiming the sparrowhawk for his own lady.

"You shall not have it," said Geraint. "I have a lady who is more beautiful and comely by far; her lineage is nobler, and it is she who ought to take the sparrow-hawk."

"We will fight for it," said the Knight of the Sparrowhawk, "to see who wins."

It was a strange sight: Geraint on horseback wearing old, heavy, rusty armour and the Knight of the Sparrowhawk with the sun dancing on his helm and harness. They fought fierce-ly, breaking spears as they were handed to them. When the Knight of the Sparrowhawk had the upper hand his troop shouted for joy and when Geraint had the upper hand the old man and his wife rejoiced. But the old man saw that the jousting could continue until dusk

unless something happened to decide matters.

He gave Geraint his best spear, the one given to him on the day he became a knight. Geraint spurred his horse on and attacked boldly. He struck his opponent hard with his spear so that the knight's shield split in two and he fell off his horse to the ground.

Geraint dismounted quickly. In the twinkling of an eye they were both on their feet, their swords flashing in the sun. They fought until their armour was broken, and until they were nearly blind as the blood and sweat ran into their eyes. It was a mighty combat.

At last, Geraint saw his chance. He struck the knight on the crown of his head until his helmet broke in two, the flesh and skin of his head were cut and the sword sank into his skull. The knight fell to his knees and called for mercy; he was thrown onto his horse and sent off to Gwenhwyfar to apologise to her maid.

Geraint, of course, won the sparrowhawk.

Enchanted by these old tales?
Why not learn to read them in Welsh?
The original Welsh version
is available at the same price.
We also publish a range of really painless
Welsh language tutors.
For a full list of publications,
send now for your free copy
of our 80-page Catalogue.

Y LOLFA
TALYBONT
CEREDIGION
CYMRU
SY24 5HE
ffôn (0970) 832 304
ffacs 832 782